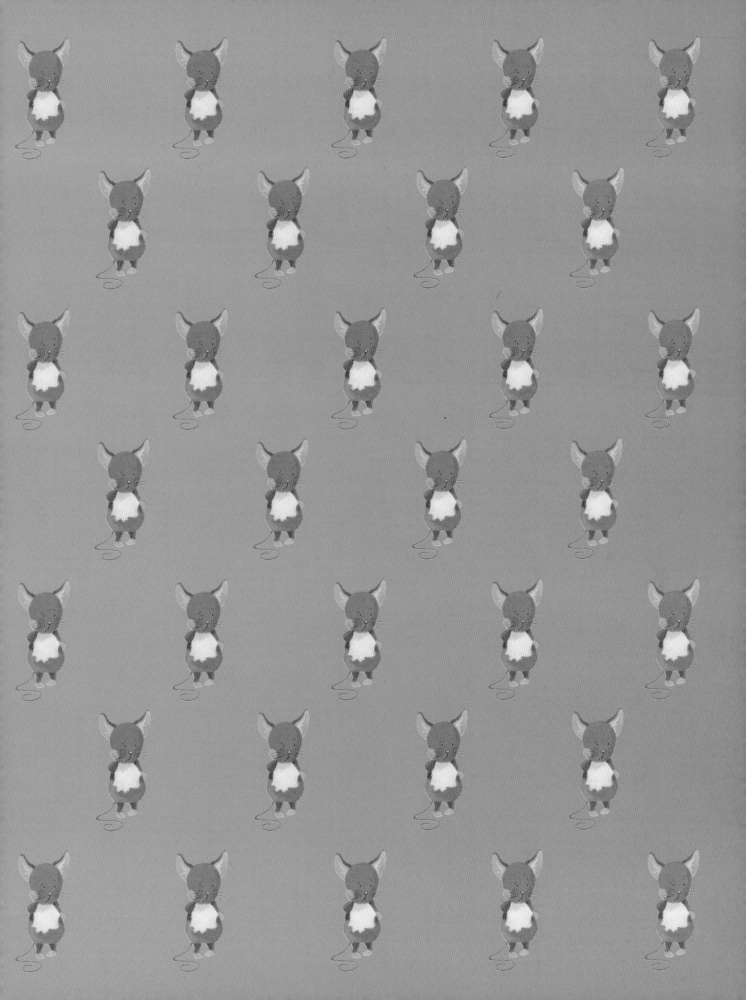

Brimax Publishing

1 Centre Road, Scoresby
Victoria 3179 Australia
Email: publishing@brimax.com.au

© Brimax Publishing, 2002
All rights reserved

ISBN 978 1 85854 725 1

Printed in China 5 4 3
A CIP catalogue record for this book is available
from the British library.

Quiet as a Mouse

BRIMAX

It was a very exciting morning in the Mouse House
when three little envelopes plopped onto the doormat.
"A party!" cried Holly and Polly, tearing open
their invitations. "We'll all have a great time."
But Molly did not agree with her sisters. She was so
shy that she blushed if another mouse so much
as twitched his whiskers at her.
"I can't possibly go!" she squeaked.

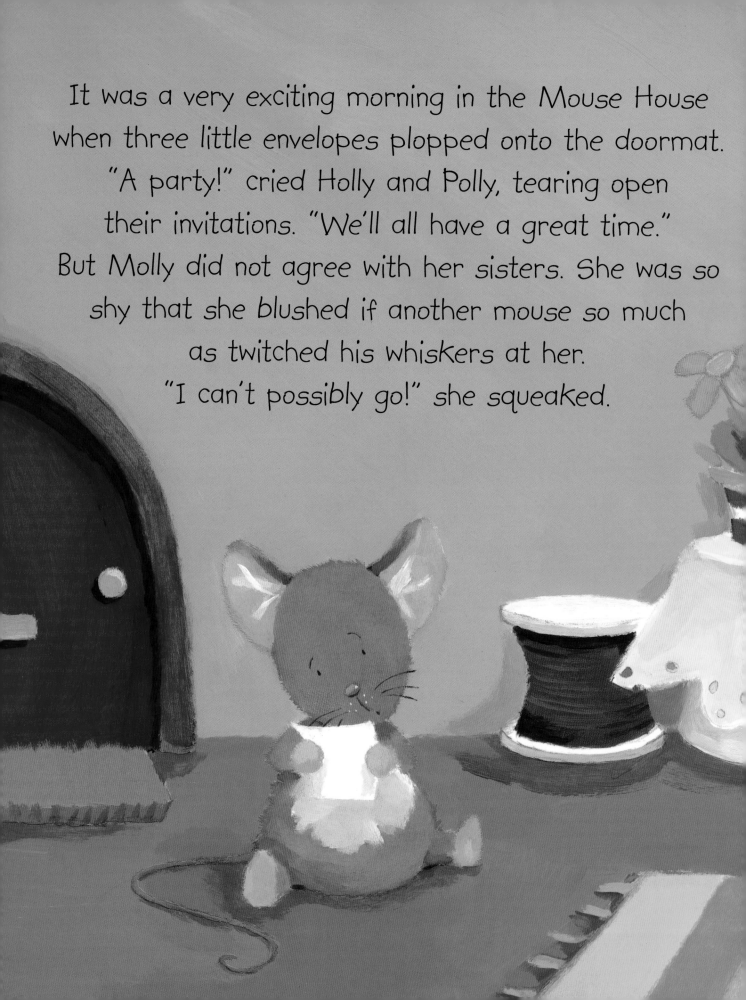

"You poor thing," said Holly, when she saw Molly.
Her whole face was covered in big, red spots.
"Are you ill?" asked Polly.
"I really don't think that I should go to the
party now," said Molly weakly.
"Oh, you'll be fine," said Mother,
"as long as you wash those spots off first."
She smiled and picked up the red crayon that
Molly had used to draw the spots.

While her sisters got ready for the party,
Molly desperately tried to think of another plan.
She decided to hide where nobody could find her.
Crawling under her bed, Molly curled up into a tiny ball.
"Molly, where are you?" called her sisters.
She held her breath and kept very, very still.

It was very dusty underneath Molly's
bed, and a piece of fluff tickled her nose.
Soon she could not hold back any longer.
"AH-CHOO!" she sneezed loudly.
"AH-CHOO! AH-CHOO! AH-CHOO!"

"We know where you are," said Holly and Polly
as they peeked under the bed.
"What are you doing?" they asked, giggling.
Feeling silly, Molly crawled out from under her
bed. There must be something else she could do!

"Hurry up, Molly," said Mother, when she saw her sitting on her bed. "It's almost time for the party." Molly just sat there, looking forlorn. "What's the matter?" asked Mother. Molly held up a piece of paper. It read, "I can't possibly go to the party. I have lost my squeak." "Oh, dear," tutted Mother. "That is a shame. I'll go and get some medicine for you."

"Poor you," said Holly, hiding a smile.
"Mother's medicine tastes really horrible."
"I'm glad I don't have to take it," said Polly.
"We're going to have so much fun at the party."

Molly thought for a little while.
Then she gave a little cough and whispered,
"Actually, I think my squeak has just come back.
Perhaps I will go to the party after all."
"Don't worry, we'll stay with you the whole time,"
said her sisters.

When they arrived at the party, Molly, Holly, and Polly were soon surrounded by lots of other little mice. "Remember what you promised," Molly squeaked, feeling her cheeks getting redder and redder and hotter and hotter. "Please don't leave me by myself."

"We promise," said Holly and Polly.

"Oh, I wish I was at home," Molly whispered.

Music began to play and the fun began. Molly
was soon caught up in a group of dancing mice.
"Oh, no!" she gasped.
Molly looked around nervously for her sisters,
but soon her feet began to move to
the music. Around and around she whirled
and twirled with the other mice.
"Where is she?" asked Holly worriedly.

Just then, Molly danced past her sisters.
"This party is fun!" she called.
"Why don't you two join in?"

Forgetting about being shy, Molly
soon made lots of new friends.

"I can't believe that this is our shy little sister,"
said Polly proudly, as Molly joined in
a game of blind man's bluff.
Wearing a blindfold, Molly searched for the
other mice, bumping into things as she went.
"Got you!" she cried, finding someone
hiding behind a tree.

"Let's play another game!" suggested Molly.
"What should we play?" asked her new friends.
Molly thought for a while, then exclaimed,
"I know! How about musical chairs?"
The little mice ran round and round a row of chairs.

When the music stopped, Molly rushed to find a seat but ended up sitting on the ground! "Whoops!" she said with a giggle.

When it was time to leave, Molly was sad to go.
"I wish we could stay longer," she said with a sigh.
"There will be other parties," Polly assured her.
"I must say goodbye to everyone,"
said Molly, rushing back.

Polly and Holly had to lead Molly from the party.
"Bye, everyone!" called Molly.
"See you again soon."

Back home, Molly told Mother all about the
wonderful time they had had at the party.
"We danced and played games and made lots
of new friends," she reported enthusiastically.
"I knew you would enjoy it," said Mother.
"Molly was the life of the party," said Holly and Polly.
"I had so much fun," said Molly,
"I'm not so shy after all."

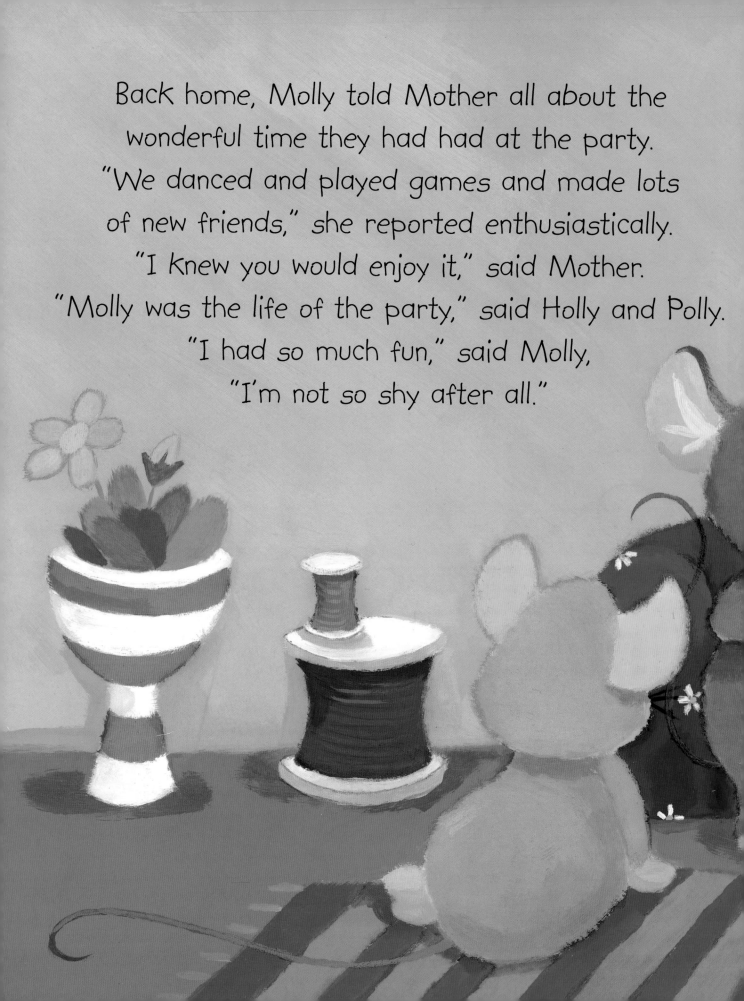

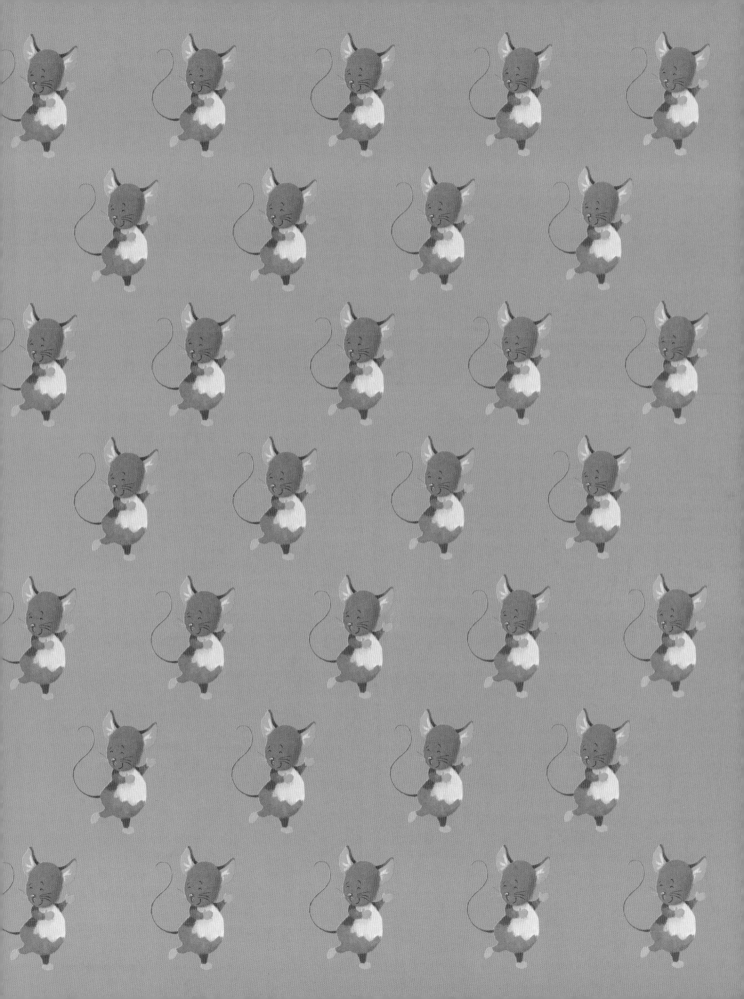